BABY BLUES

"Jimmy!" His mom   ⊔
back down.

"Jimmy, listen. Th

ing at me like she re⎯⎯ ⎯⎯⎯ ⎯⎯⎯ ⎯⎯ ⎯ ⎯⎯ beginning to relax a little.

"People are gonna . . . people'll talk, wanna know
what's up. We're all going to get the same. We gotta
deal with it together."

Jimmy's not having any. He slams the door and
starts running. In his workboots. He hasn't even got
sneakers.

I know just what he's thinking. We been through it
so many times, how there's no way. Nothing to do.
How he's got a dumb job, no high school, no money,
how maybe his mom can take the baby, or one of her
sisters, or even Frankie. But then what happens if we
want the kid back? And the kid'll have parents, I
mean the guys who brought him up and stuff. He
might say, where you been, Dad? Why'd you dump
me?

So we give it away—our kid?

Baby Blues

A Novel By

Hope Wurmfeld

PUFFIN BOOKS

PUFFIN BOOKS
Published by the Penguin Group
Penguin Books USA Inc., 375 Hudson Street, New York, New York 10014, U.S.A.
Penguin Books Ltd, 27 Wrights Lane, London W8 5TZ, England
Penguin Books Australia Ltd, Ringwood, Victoria, Australia
Penguin Books Canada Ltd, 10 Alcorn Avenue, Toronto, Ontario, Canada M4V 3B2
Penguin Books (N.Z.) Ltd, 182-190 Wairau Road, Auckland 10, New Zealand

Penguin Books Ltd, Registered Offices: Harmondsworth, Middlesex, England

First published in the United States of America by Viking,
a division of Penguin Books USA Inc., 1992
Published in Puffin Books, 1995

1 3 5 7 9 10 8 6 4 2

THE LIBRARY OF CONGRESS HAS CATALOGED THE VIKING EDITION AS FOLLOWS:
Wurmfeld, Hope Herman.
Baby blues / by Hope Herman Wurmfeld.
p. cm.
Summary: After her father's death, Annie is forced to make some hard choices
about her life and her evolving relationship with her best friend Jimmie.
ISBN 0-670-84151-X
[1. Friendship—Fiction. 2. Death—Fiction.] I. Title.
PZ7.W9627Bab 1992 [Fic]—dc20 92-5828 CIP AC

Puffin Books ISBN 0-14-034870-0

Printed in the United States of America

For Zelda, my mom

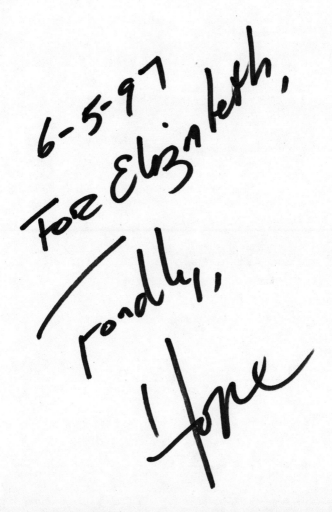

6-5-97

For Elizabeth,

Fondly,

Hope

1 *"Pop, you need anything, Pop? Can I turn on the TV? You wanna little coffee?"* I'm late. The school bus is coming and I'm afraid I'll miss it again. Another day without high school. The teachers don't really care, though. One less kid to worry about.

"Bye, Pop. See you later." No answer. His eyes are blank. A small voice in back of my head's saying he really ain't good today.

School is only a half a day. Some holiday or something. I come home and my brother Frankie's eighteen-wheeler is out front and him and my other brother, Kenny, are there in their work clothes. My brothers never sit around the living room with their work clothes on, so right away I know something's up.

Frankie says, "I think you better sit." He sits down next to me and takes my arm. "Pop's bad, real bad. You can't do nothing. He's going."

I run upstairs to Pop's room and we look at each other and it's like he don't see me. There's nothing there.

If it hadn't been for Jimmy, I don't know how I would've got through the next few months. By the time Pop died, I missed so much school, I quit going. Jimmy was the only friend I had to talk to.

Jimmy's my boyfriend and sometimes he don't get along too good with his parents. He gives them a real hard time. Like he walks out of his house even when they tell him he can't go and he runs with his friends, like R.B. and Slug and Toker. They don't steal or stick people, but there's those who think they do, especially R.B. He got this reputation. Jimmy says he's tough, but not cold crazy. R.B. ain't mean.

R.B.'s his best friend, short for Rainbow. Jimmy's ma hates R.B. cause R.B. quit school last fall and so did Jimmy. All R.B. thinks about is graffiti and trains. Well, not trains no more, but walls and bridges and just any place where there's space to draw. Jimmy thinks he's the greatest.

Sometimes Jimmy don't come home until late. And his mom'll wait up and yell and he'll walk right past her and up the stairs and slam the door of his room.

First time I saw Jimmy to speak to him, it was about a year ago. No, it was maybe just before school started. I'm sitting on a bench, not really sitting on it, sort of on the back of it with my legs hanging off. I was at the mall in front of the video arcade.

And Jimmy comes out with Rainbow and Slug and a bunch of other guys. I knew who he was already because of his eyes. They're blue like the sky or a clear blue marble you can see right through. He looks right at me. So I go up to him. I know some of the girls he hangs out with. They think he's older. He kind of shows off. He thinks he's so cool and stuff with those eyes.

And I know that his girlfriend is thinking of getting rid of him. You know, kicking him off. I know about it, but I don't say nothing to him. I ask him if he's got wheels. He goes, ''Yeah.''

''Do you got a license?''

''No.''

So I say, ''Well, how come you hang around with *her* then?'' She's the kind that's into motorcycles and cars and someone who can drive. I was really mean.

After that I seen him in the hall sometimes. We

went to the same junior high. And he must've followed me home from school because he knew where I live.

Then I'm at the mall one night with some girl-friends. Jimmy and me still ain't spoke except for that time in front of the video arcade. When I see him, I feel myself getting red. I know I been snotty to him. I guess I like him already.

So I go up to him and say, "How come you never say hello to nobody?"

"I don't know nobody," he says.

"*I* don't know nobody and I'm talking to you. You can talk to anybody here and they just . . . and it's okay." He's laughing and bumping into me with his shoulder, and then I bump his shoulder real hard and he makes like he's mad at me and we both start running out onto the blacktop where the cars are parked. And then we're walking out to the road.

Then we started going out. And he began to talk, like, tell me stuff. He liked me.

2 *So me and Jimmy start hanging out. We're at the mall playing video games at the arcade.* I keep messing up my car.

R.B. comes in and him and Jimmy go talk in a corner and they're looking over at me, and so then R.B. and Jimmy come over where I'm standing and Rainbow says, "Wanna go bombing?"

I'm thinking, yeah, cool, but I'm a little scared like this ain't kid stuff. This is like, if you get caught, forget it—god, my brother Frankie'll be mad. But, Jimmy really wants to go. So I'm saying, "Yeah, why not."

Bombing's when you do graffiti. Rainbow's part of a gang, a crew called Spectrum, "Spec" for short. They do all this graffiti stuff. It used to be you go to the train yard at night, but they did something to the trains. The paint comes off and it isn't fun no more. So Spec crew, they do billboards and under bridges and stuff along the highway.

We go with R.B. We're gonna meet Slug and Toker at the bridge. We have bikes, but R.B. makes us come with him in Slug's pickup. So we get to a place where he pulls over and we leave the truck and walk and then we climb over a barbed-wire fence. Signs all over say: KEEP OUT, GOVERNMENT PROPERTY. TRESPASS-ERS WILL BE PROSECUTED.

Rainbow sticks a spray can in my hand and I start spraying. It feels good. I'm getting into yellow spray paint. I'm not even thinking about Keep Out signs anymore. Just yellow paint all over the walls.

Jimmy's got blue and Toker red and we're all spray-ing and really into it.

Rainbow's got a fat black marker and he's making these real fresh squiggles and lines. He's writing *SHA-BAZ*, and *BOOM*, and then he writes *AR#@*. And then a whole bunch of stuff I don't read. Not like the rest of us—just playing, just messing. Rainbow's stuff is real cool, real pretty, crazy lines—thin and thick and curvy and your eyeballs really get into it. He makes a skull with fire coming out of its eyes only it's not fire, it's a rainbow. That's his thing—his tag. Nobody else does it or they get in trouble with the crew. It's like Frankie on the CB. He's got a name everybody knows him by.

R.B.'s stopping. He's kind of listening or something and he's saying, "Yo, man, let's split." He puts a finger over his mouth so we catch his drift: Keep still and let's go.

R.B.'s kind of crouching down, so we do, too, and then we're crawling behind Slug and Toker. It's dark and we can't see too good. We're back at the truck. No R.B.

I'm real scared. My stomach's doing loops. Then we hear something in the bushes and we see Rainbow limping over to the truck. He's got blood on his shirt. I can't tell if it's his or what.

Slug starts the truck and hits the bluegrass station. Whoever drives gets to pick. When we're back in our neighborhood, he pulls over and Toker takes out some weed. "Annie?"

I take a drag and pass it.

Rainbow says, "Somebody dropped a dime on us. The Macho crew must've heard we'd be out. I hurt someone back there. They'll be coming after me. But they don't got wheels."

Slug drives me and Jimmy to get our bikes at the mall. It's a weeknight and the last movie was over an hour ago. What if the Machos are out cruising?

What if they seen us get outta the truck with Slug and Rainbow?

We get on our bikes and begin to pedal down a long hill, the only one around cause this town's mostly flat. A trucking hub, that's what Frankie calls it. It isn't so much a town, he goes, it's roads. You can get almost anywhere from here—Indiana, Michigan, Kentucky—even Florida if you want. Right now, Florida don't sound too bad. I'm about froze. My hands are numb even though I got gloves. We're really moving. We're flying through a back alley, behind the post office, through the parking lot at the supermarket, out in front of the bank, past dark houses with no lights on like they're deserted or something. And I'm hearing my bike wheels whooshing around like we're maybe the last two kids in the whole world. The traffic lights are on hold—some are just blinking red. At one corner down by the hardware store, a car flicks on its lights and Jimmy and I pedal harder. It pulls out and turns at the first right. I feel my shoulders let go a little.

We're passing the cemetery where Pop is. That afternoon before Christmas when Pop went, I don't remember a lot of what happened. Somehow things got taken care of. Frankie made the arrangements. The coffin looked so small. My brothers said it hardly weighed nothing. Pop was big, but he sorta shrunk when he got leukemia. My aunt and my brothers and me and Jimmy. That's all there was. Pop didn't have no friends. The sun was shining that day, but I kept thinking like it was dark out or something.

I'm following Jimmy and we're both riding kinda by instinct. I know the roads and the potholes real good cause I been riding my bike around this town every day almost forever. I feel safe riding at night, like the dark'll protect me.

We're close to my house and Jimmy slows down next to the wall. The wall is this thing in the neighborhood that kinda spooks us out. When we were little, we made up stories about ghosts and stuff and we'd run until we got past it. The house behind the wall—no kids in there or nothing. And in winter no footprints in the snow, like no one ever goes in or out.

We're at the wall and Jimmy's stopping and he gets a toe-hold between the bricks and he's up there. I try to climb it, but keep slipping off.

So we both sit in the snow leaning against the bricks. He's making a snowball, so I make a snowball and then we start throwing them. And then he does this thing all the little kids do—they try to grab you and wash your face with snow.

He grabs me—at first I'm not expecting nothing, like maybe he's gonna kiss me or something—and then, he starts pushing snow in my face and we're both laughing and I'm grabbing his arms and before we know it, we're hugging each other.

Then, he's kissing me. And I'm kissing him right back. And it's, I don't know, it's like I don't care what happens to me. I can stay like this forever—his mouth on my mouth, his smell, sort of minty like Wrigley's, and like a garage.

I don't know how long we're doing this. I stop thinking about Pop, about whether Frankie's home and waiting up for me and getting mad. It's just Jimmy, me and Jimmy. Then he puts his hand under my coat and I feel him getting kind of crazy. He's breathing different.

It's our first time really kissing and stuff. And I'm scared—scared to do *It* and scared not to. Scared that he'll kick me off if I don't. I wasn't . . . I just never thought . . .

So he's saying, "Come on, Annie, let me. I know you want to."

And I'm, "I don't know."

Jimmy's just lying there against the wall with his arms folded across his chest. I can't tell if he's mad or what. He ain't saying nothing. I don't know how long we were that way. And I'm thinking how can it be so great one minute and so awful the next. I feel cold and sort of creepy.

Then something happens, something weird. Jimmy

grabs my hand. We're looking at each other. We're spooked, but we ain't sure why. We hear something or maybe it's just the trees, or, or . . . The street light is doing this thing. It's totally dark and then it ain't, like it's possessed or going whack or something.

Jimmy pulls me up. "We're outta here." I'm on my bike. My heart's pounding so hard I'm scared it's gonna jump outta my chest. All I can think about is getting away from there—from the wall and the dark. I keep seeing R.B.'s shirt with blood all over it. I don't hear nothing till I'm on my corner, in front of Ray's Pizza and Rosie's and the supermarket.

Everything's lit, even though there's no people. I'm leaning on my bike near the fence in front of the market trying to breathe.

And then we're standing outside my house not saying nothing, just looking at each other. And Jimmy's brushing stuff outta my hair. "Annie, it's . . . it's okay. Don't . . ."

I open my front door—the truck's not here and Kenny sleeps in the living room when he has a fight with his wife. No one's there. I take Jimmy's hand and pull him in.

3 *He must have been watching me cause he takes the cheese off the top shelf that I ain't reaching and tosses it into my basket.* Rainbow was working at Sparky's Paint Store so I don't get what he's doing in the supermarket on my corner in a white apron with his hair pulled back tight.

"Sparky dissed me," he goes, like he's inside my head. "They, uh, maybe they was wondering what was happening to the spray paint." He's laughing, but it's coming out of his chest from way down—

and his eyes they're just dark, like he pulled down a shade. You can't tell what he's thinking.

I don't know how he got me to ride. I just said, okay, just like that, even though Frankie's driving a hundred miles out of his way for a home-cooked meal tonight. R.B.'s revving the Harley and we're flying through the streets, running like we own the wind and the sky. My hair is wild and I got hold of his leather jacket like it's a magic carpet.

We're going to his house. Jimmy says nobody's been to R.B.'s house, not Toker or Slug. Not even Jimmy. People say funny things about R.B.'s house like he lives in a cave or in some awful place just because they ain't seen it. And they say his mom is scary or something and that he hasn't got a father, his father ran away when he was little.

Inside it's dark and I'm not sure where I'm putting my feet. There's a light on somewhere. We walk closer and I see someone. I see someone sitting curled up in a large chair. When my eyes get used to the dark, I see a woman with big dark eyes that catch the light of the small lamp next to her. I know those eyes.

I hear R.B. speaking real low and gentle. "I brought a friend, Mama. Her name's Annie. She's Jimmy's girl, Mama."

R.B. talks different when he's talking to his mama.

I go near to shake hands, but R.B.'s mom just sits there looking straight ahead. I sort of have the creeps.

"Mama's blind," Rainbow goes. "She can't see but she knows a lot of things. She listens to me watching, she listens to me dreaming about color."

He puts my hand on his mama's. I can't believe this is happening, that I'm meeting R.B.'s mom. I heard such weird stuff about black magic and spells— nothing about a sweet, blind mama.

She's holding my hand between two of her own, pressing my palm with her thumbs. Her hand moves to my face and runs over my nose, my eyes, my hair. Her touch is like she's seeing me with her hands. She still isn't saying anything. She's kind of talking to herself. "Beautiful," she's going, "very beautiful." Then she got my hand again but something's different, her expression. She's quiet for a long time and then she's saying, "If you need to talk, come to me. I am here for you." It's like she's seeing something else. I got the shivers.

———

It's after dark. Sunny, Frankie's girlfriend, she's not here yet, but I hear Frankie. He revs the engine twice and blows his horn when he gets home, so I know it's Frankie and so does the whole block. The rig's in the supermarket lot, but he parks the cab out front.

Frankie hugs me, drops his bag on the floor, and opens the door to the frig all at the same time.

And I'm, "I ain't so good. I burned the spaghetti sauce." For some reason I feel like crying.

"Don't worry, princess, it'll be great. It's home cooked!" The beer can hisses when Frankie pulls the tab. "And it ain't *ain't*."

Most of the time I laugh and tease him back and say only dummies smoke cigarettes or something. But tonight, I don't know. Maybe I'm just tired. Me and Jimmy, we, I ain't sure I get what's so great about making out—Jimmy saying my name over and over—and after when we hold each other. I gotta talk . . . but, I just don't, I don't know nobody who knows about, who knows about stuff.

"Hey, sugar. What's the matter?" Frankie takes a long slug of Coors, "You pissed about something?"

The doorbell rings and I'm grateful not to have to talk, not to have to make something up.

Frankie's in a good mood. He opens the front door with his eyes closed and his arms wide, "Sunny! Kiss me, lover!"

"Sure thing, faggot." Frankie's eyes open fast. It's Rainbow and he's standing there holding my scarf.

Frankie has this look on his face and I know that look. When he was little and he'd see some kid getting it in the school yard or something, Frankie'd go nuts. He don't like to be messed with and he don't like to see other kids messed with. He's looking at R.B. like, who is the kid on my doorstep calling me a faggot.

All of a sudden I'm seeing R.B. the way, well, like Pop would've seen him—a leather motorcycle jacket over his shoulders, and long stringy black hair tied in a ponytail only it don't stay right and falls over his eyes. And he's real tall, much taller than Frankie. And skinny. He has a scar on his chin and a tattoo on his arm—same as his tag—a skull with rainbow fire coming out the eyes. And the way his arms are folded, he's sticking that tattoo right in Frankie's face.

I'm looking at Frankie and I'm looking at Rainbow and I'm scared. I mean, this is Jimmy's best friend. I'm praying Frankie don't do something stupid.

After that Frankie don't want to hear about R.B. It's like Frankie just don't make sense when it comes to Rainbow. I tell Frankie it's not like he thinks, but Frankie don't listen. Frankie acts jealous of Rainbow or something. Jimmy's my boyfriend, so how come he ain't jealous of Jimmy? Sometimes I think I just get in the way of Frankie. Like if he didn't have me to look out for maybe him and Sunny'd get married.

Even Jimmy isn't so sure he likes R.B. hanging out. I keep telling him we're friends, just friends. It's not like a boyfriend—like I don't, we don't kiss or anything. The only time I touch him is when we're on the Harley. But Frankie doesn't want to hear about me riding. He thinks I do it just to get him pissed. So if I ride, I'm not talking about it.

4 *I gained a little weight. Not so much you could* *see anything. After I eat or something I gotta undo my top button.* Me and the guys some nights we go down to the lake. There're signs all over the place: KEEP OUT! NO TRESPASSING! like under the bridge. Frankie says they're gonna build condos or a hospital or something, but so far it don't look like nobody's there.

Sometimes me and Jimmy just go off by ourselves. But mostly we make a fire with twigs and stuff and do weed and hang out. Sparks go up in the sky like Christmas lights. But the water's all black and still, you can't see anything there. The only light's a red glow from town and that's sort of far. When it's really hot we swim and dare each other who's gonna go first. We don't have suits so the guys look the other way when it's my turn. But like last week, I don't know, I feel kind of—well, I'm not fat or anything. I just don't feel a lot like going in.

One night we're hanging out with Slug and Toker—passing weed and watching the moon float. R.B.'s going, "I'm making a hit: bombing and stuff, and the train is all silver, real shiny and smooth, totally awesome."

With Rainbow sometimes you don't know if it's real or a dream or a little of both. So now he's talking how he's taking pictures of his tag and the flash on his Polaroid it splits the sky like lightning or something.

Toker's fidgety. He just can't sit still. He gets up and starts running a ways along the edge of the water and goes, "Rainbow?"

"Yo."

"We're there? Right? Us guys? And Annie?"

"Sure thing, man."

"So throw me some red." Rainbow makes like he's tossing a can of spray paint. Slugger gets into it. He runs out to a rock across from Toker.

"Over here, dude. Look at this. Got our name on it. This rock, it's going, 'Paint me!' "

R.B. grabs him from behind and Slug kind of spins around with his fists up. "Yo, man, whatcha . . . ?"

"No beef, just fixing your bandana, man . . . paint fumes." R.B. pats Slug's arm, "No beef, honest."

I'm pretending to zap R.B. with spray paint. And I'm . . . I'm thinking of the scariest thing I can think of.

"Machos!" I go. R.B. turns fast and pretends he's aiming a piece. "Let's blow 'em away!" Jimmy runs over and faces R.B. with his arms straight out on R.B.'s shoulders kind of pushing him. "Hey man, it ain't worth getting killed over."

Then Jimmy makes like he's Dog Face, the Macho's head honcho. He kind of stretches his neck the way Dog Face does and sticks out his lower lip like a bulldog and goes, "Oh, please. Please don't hurt me. I'll be good. I promise I'll be good." Jimmy and R.B. start punching each other, not for real, and crack up laughing. Jimmy really looks like Dog Face when he does that stuff with his lip.

The bottom of my jeans are wet and I'm out of breath. The fire's low and we're sitting close. All you can see is our chins. We look like monsters or something.

And Rainbow's going, "So I made this hit and I hear a sound. It ain't human. I think it's maybe one of them dogs in the yard where the trains turn around. So I look and there's this thing—like nothing I ever seen. And it's after me. It's breathing in a crazy way. Its eyes are burning into me. I try to run, but I'm stuck in mud or something. I can't move.''

By now we're really creeped out. I'm almost sitting on Jimmy, and Slug and Toker are so close on the other side of Rainbow they look like one huge person with two heads. And I'm worried maybe Frankie'll have a fit or something cause it's getting kinda late.

This is the crazy part, what really freaked me. R.B., he's saying my name.

"Annie." He goes, "Annie!" His voice is thin, high like Jimmy's kid sister. It don't sound like him. I can't tell if he's fooling around or high or what. He sure isn't smiling. His eyes . . . it's like he's seeing something we ain't seeing. It makes my skin crawl. He stops talking and gets real quiet like he's still inside his story, like we're not there.

Then he looks at me, right in my face with those crazy eyes. His voice is back to normal, only now he's whispering, "It's you, Annie. You and Jimmy. You're there in the yard, only I can't see you. I gotta get you out of there, only I can't move my legs."

We're passing weed. Rainbow takes a long drag and kind of shakes his head like he's waking up or something. I'm going, "Well, do we make it outta there or what?" Rainbow's not saying anything, just sitting quiet. I feel strange, like I don't know, like I had this feeling in my gut all the time Rainbow's talking, this feeling we're not alone.

"Something's out there," I go.

R.B.'s head kinda jerks up. "Annie, don't say stuff like that. That ain't funny."

And then they're standing around us kinda in a circle, four, maybe five guys. Did they hear R.B.'s story? They step in closer. I'm piss scared. R.B. and Jimmy stand. R.B.'s eyes are big, dark—you can't see nothing in them. Jimmy got his hands in his pockets, sort of ready, sort of tough. Toker and Slug are standing between Jimmy and R.B. It's like the blackness is alive. I think I see two guys from Macho crew and then some others. I'm not sure. We ain't outnumbered, if you count me. At least R.B.'s the biggest.

There's a lot of loud talking. R.B. and Jimmy go over and say something that me and Toker and Slug can't hear. When they come back, they ain't saying nothing. The other guys leave. It was too easy. I don't get it.

Jimmy told me later Rainbow was gonna go down where the trains go at night . . . and it'd be just R.B. and Dog Face.

5 *I prayed I was wrong, that I was just getting fat or something, that it would go away. I was scared Jimmy would leave me.* I didn't think of using anything and Jimmy didn't either so this is on both our heads. I wouldn't just blame Jimmy.

I went the whole summer. But, when I began to . . . when I knew for sure, I'm thinking I gotta do something. I know it's crazy. Like I don't do nothing for so long and now . . . now I'm really scared.

So I'm at Rosie's Deli for coffee and I'm thinking what to do, at the counter—pouring the milk, I like it light, and saying hi and stuff to Rosie. Rosie's old, like fifty or something, and her place's been there forever. She loves to, you know, gab and stuff, and listen to all the blah, blah that people come in with.

So I'm trying to stay away from Rosie. And I see Frankie's driving buddy, Beans. That's what they call him on the CB cause he used to live in Boston.

I say, "Hey, Beanie, I gotta talk to Frankie. You know where he's at?"

"Sure thing, Princess."

Beanie always calls me Princess like I'm eight years old. He should only know. I make a face, but I sort of like it when he calls me that. Like I feel safe or something when he calls me that, I don't know why.

I always looked young. I got good hair, sort of light brown and curly with a lot of red in it, and I'm skinny, at least I was. Now I wear these big shirts and sweaters kinda open so you can't see nothing. I ain't bad-looking, I guess.

Beans pays and we walk back behind the supermarket to his truck. He boosts me into the cab and starts calling on the CB.

"Roadrunner, come in, Roadrunner. Beanpot to Roadrunner, let's hear it."

The truck is warm and I'm starting to feel drowsy, so I climb into the back where Beans sleeps when he's not driving and lie down on a blue blanket with horses' heads traced in white at the top. I used to love to ride with Frankie when I was little. I even thought I'd be a truck driver when I grew up. Nobody to boss you around, tell you what to do.

I need to think what I'm gonna tell Frankie. How I'm gonna tell him. But I keep drifting off. All I see is graffiti, big yellow and blue tags: *SPEC, SHABAZ, JIMMY LOVES ANNIE,* and Rainbow's mom that time at his house. She knew something, I don't know how, even before the summer. God, when I think about the summer. Sometimes at the diner helping Rosie work breakfast, I'd get so nauseous from the smell of bacon and home fries. I never eat before lunch. So I'm thinking this is just a little worse. But it was different. I should've seen it. And that button that kept falling off the top of my jeans.

I must've dozed off cause the next thing I know Bean's got the Jake brake on, the airbrakes, they make a racket, and he's pulling the semi into a Perlis truckstop. I don't know where we are. I ain't been watching the road too good.

Frankie's Freightliner is parked with about ten other big rigs. He's got a flatbed loaded with steel. I only done this once before when we had an emergency with Pop so Frankie knows something's up.

We sit at a table with a telephone. Cigarette smoke's coming at me front and back and I'm getting nauseous and trying not to be sick. Frankie's not talking. He's just looking at me, real serious. I know he's thinking, this better be good.

The waitress comes and Frankie orders a coffee and fried chicken with mashed potatoes and gravy and green beans. The waitress's saying the green beans are the best, special today. I'm feeling sicker by the minute. I can't imagine sitting and watching anyone eat all that food.

I go, "Just water," when the waitress looks at me. Frankie tells the waitress to bring me some tea and blueberry pie. He sees I'm not good. He always thinks blueberry pie'll make me feel better.

This is tougher than I thought. It's like Frankie's the oldest and he always looked out for me when I was growing up. I suppose he loves me and all, but we don't always talk to each other so good. He still thinks I'm a little kid just like Beanie does. Frankie's kid sister.

The waitress brings the coffee and the tea and pie. I take a sip of tea and put it down with a shudder. It's too hot. Frankie's looking right at me. He reaches across the table and touches my arm.

"I been watching you. I been watching you since Pop. And you're not right.

"Annie?" I'm looking at the table. I can't look him in the eye. The waitress is putting down the stuff in a hurry. I'm watching her painted fingernails and these spots on the backs of her hands. Frankie's getting pissed.

When I open my mouth, I mean, when I'm telling him, when I'm saying the words, I burst into tears. I ain't holding nothing back. Frankie's hearing it.

Frankie hands me a paper napkin for my nose. And he's looking at me and shaking his head, like he don't believe it.

"A jerk, a great, big stupid jerk, that's what you are, kiddo." Frankie's really mad. I never seen him so mad. Not cause I'm pregnant. He's not mad about that. It's cause I didn't come to him. That's what really hurts him. I didn't trust him. He can't believe I waited so long to tell him.

He's yelling at me for not getting one of those home pregnancy tests. He says I could've found out right away. The minute I thought something. I know he's right.

He knows more about this stuff than I thought. He said I should have at least talked to one person, come to one person—him or my aunt or R.B.'s mom or anybody. But I just couldn't. God, I'm so dumb. At least Pop didn't have to know.

⬥

We had this appointment for the doctor, me and Frankie, and we go in and he examines me and then I go in the waiting room. I'm pretty sure I'll be able to get rid of it—no way am I gonna have this baby. Frankie's got his arm around my shoulder and keeps patting me. I think he's trying to make himself feel better, too. I been putting him through a lot lately.

After that night with Rainbow and Dog Face at the train yard, Frankie went down to the police station with Jimmy to bail Rainbow out. Jimmy says Dog Face wasn't alone. Some of the Machos showed up after they got started. Jimmy's seeing it from behind a box car. He's just running out when the cops show up and cuff everybody. Jimmy don't know how they knew. He says Dog Face went back on his word. One thing that drives Jimmy really crazy, it's when you go back on your word. Him and Rainbow talk about it a lot. He says it's the worst thing.

The door to the examining room opens and the doctor comes out and says there's nothing to do. I'm over six months. I gotta carry it.

See, we was going that day to have it aborted. Frankie knew where. We would've done it without telling no one, not even Jimmy. But it was twenty-four weeks already and the doctor says it would've been a health risk. They could've lost me.

So when I hear this, I start to really cry. Jimmy's gonna be mad. He's gonna blow me off. That was the worst. My best friend's gonna blow me off. Frankie's got me by the shoulders and is sort of holding me up. I can hardly stand. By this time, we're in front of the doctor's office and a kid on a bike has his neck screwed around to watch us and a lady with shopping bags is looking at me like she thinks I'm a nut case or something.

So Frankie is like, we have to tell Jimmy and his family and my brother Kenny. I just can't do it. Frankie worries about the family, but I worry about Jimmy. No one else can tell Jimmy.

It's gray and there's kind of a drizzle and my hair's frizzy, not curly. It's one of those days the leaves smell sort of rotten and when you run, you can skid even in sneakers.

Jimmy had dreams before he dropped out, like he'd be drafted by the big-league scouts right out of high school. He'd hit the ball outta the park and the coach would act mad cause there's no money for balls. But he really wasn't. He tried to get him not to quit school.

So I'm walking, not really looking at nothing and I hear the bat. It's Jimmy and Slug and Toker and some guys in the back by his house. A big empty lot. Kids play ball and mess around there and stuff. There's nothing there but weeds and beer cans and old condoms and broken bottles and stuff. It's kind of a mess.

I climb over this broke-down chain fence and all this used-up stuff that's stuck in the corners.

Jimmy sees me and calls time out. Then he takes one look at me and tells the guys, "See ya later." I guess I look pretty bad.

He's running over to me and I'm thinking, god, he's so cute. His blond hair is kinda curly and in the rain, it's shiny, and he's sorta tan from working outside so his eyes look really blue.

"So?" he's standing next to me.

I say, "Well . . ." like I'm really scared. It's a different scared from when the Machos found us at the cove. That night I was scared in my guts. Now it's my guts and my head, too. I'm cold all over. My heart is pounding and I can hardly stand up.

"So, uh, what's with your hair?"

I touch my head and say something stupid like it's raining, but he's still looking at me. And I'm thinking, like, I busted up his ball game and I'm still not talking.

So then he goes, "Wanna walk?"

He starts walking in front of me down this street that ends in a used-car dump. We're sitting on a pile of wrecked tires and I'm staring at these smashed-up dead Fords and Chevies with broke windshields and stuff and I just say it right out. I can't keep it in no more.

"I'm gonna have a baby. I can't do nothing, like have an abortion or something, it's too late. And I'm telling you right away, I ain't gonna marry you. No way am I gonna marry you."

Jimmy's looking at me and even though he's tan, he's pale, and his eyes go kind of weird and dark and he's so still, quiet. I never seen him so quiet, cause he's mostly, you know, moving all the time, but now he's froze.

Even his voice, I can hardly hear him.

He's mumbling stuff like how he did this to me and oh god, it's all his fault, and crazy stuff, like we gotta run away, go somewhere, and that he ain't gonna leave me, no matter what.

Something gets hold of me and I say, "Jimmy, listen, we're not gonna run. I got my brother. You got parents. We're not gonna run. We gotta tell 'em."

Me and Jimmy, we get off the tires and begin to walk, kind of holding each other up, sort of bumping into each other. We're just walking, not saying much, not thinking where we're going, holding hands. We're on my corner. Without thinking about it, I walked home.

The neon supermarket sign's glowing red on the rainy sidewalk. Jimmy goes in and comes out with Rainbow. We go to Rosie's and R.B.'s pushing us to the back to sit. Rosie knows about the back booth. The back booth is stay away. God, here I am again at Rosie's—I can't believe this is happening to me.

R.B. looks from me to Jimmy. When Rainbow talks, you see where Dog Face busted his tooth. "Yo, anybody home? Speak, man." He lights two cigarettes and hands one to Jimmy. Rosie puts down Cokes and walks away. Nobody's saying a lot. R.B.'s looking at me, right in my eyes. R.B. knows me pretty good by now. He can tell this is a tough one. Then he's looking at Jimmy. "Hey, man, what'd you do? Kill somebody? I mean, like I'm the one who's, you know, who's got the reputation." Rainbow almost got Jimmy to smile.

"Yeah, well, it ain't that bad, but it's . . . it's just that I'm gonna, we're gonna . . ." Jimmy's covering his face with his hands. He can't say it. Jimmy can stand up to the Macho crew when it's really tense. He's never afraid of that kind of stuff. But he just can't say that he knocked up his girlfriend.

"I'm going to have a kid," I go. "I can't do anything, it's too late. And Jimmy's afraid his dad'll beat him and that Frankie'll hate him, maybe even kill him."

R.B.'s eyes are coal. "Ain't nobody gonna hurt you, man, you hear?" I was trying to explain it to Jimmy when I told him about the kid. Frankie's not mad at anybody—only mad that I didn't tell him sooner, that I didn't talk to someone.

R.B. was really great with Jimmy. It was Jimmy we had to help cause he got parents and a kid sister. He's scared of his dad and his mom, oh, god, his mom. Jimmy, he just feels so bad.

"Thank god Pop didn't have to know about this."
If Frankie says that one more time, I'm gonna
throw up. The cigarette's smoking in the ash-
tray, and he's lighting another one. He sees me
watching.

"I'm gonna quit, princess. It's just that—"

"Don't call me that. I'm not a kid!" I'm staring at
Frankie. I think I'm yelling. I ain't sure of anything
anymore. My face is hot. I know I look awful. He
puts down the Coors, puts out his cigarette in the
sink, and takes my arm.

It's better out of the house, walking, doing something. The air feels good. The nighttime guys are
hanging out at Rosie's and the air is thick with smoke.
But it's okay, it feels better, safe somehow. Rosie
comes over with a coffee and a Coke and gives
Frankie a look like they know each other pretty good.
Frankie and Rosie—how come I never . . . I'm getting
things I ain't seen before. Frankie gets up and talks
to Rosie.

Is he telling her about me or what? He comes back
with the Yellow Pages. First we look under Baby and
that's nowhere. And then, Adoption, Adoption with
Love, Adoption Services Associates, Birth Hope—
Adoption Information and Advocacy, Downey Side,
Edwin Gould . . . the list goes on for two columns.

There's been such awful stuff, stories and stuff in the papers. Frankie's scared that these places aren't legit. Like how do we know that they really care about kids? I'm watching Frankie, but I'm not saying nothing. I just feel so tired.

Frankie lights another Camel and inhales. He says there's gotta be a place for a kid to get adopted by a family that really wants one. Maybe a family that can't have a kid of its own. There's a guy he knows, a road buddy, Pete, whose sister's a social worker. He's gonna speak to Pete.

In the end it was Frankie who found a way to take care of things. It was Frankie who told Jimmy's parents.

6 *Mackey sent Jimmy home from the garage two
days in a row. Says he ain't good for much.
He's daydreaming and he's gonna get hurt.*
So Jimmy's dad goes down to talk to Mackey, they're
army buddies from Vietnam. All Jimmy wants to do
is work on the engine of the Harley he bought off
two girls at the lake last summer. His dad says it's a
lemon.

So I'm standing in his garage and holding a dumb
flashlight so he can see into the engine. The phone
starts. Jimmy picks up in the kitchen and makes a

face when he sees what his workboots are doing to his mom's new floor.

"Who? Dad? He's not . . . I'm sorry, you got the wrong . . . What'd you say? Who's this? Slug? Hey, who? . . ." The line goes dead. "Jimmy. They says 'Jimmy' and then 'Hi, dad.' " Jimmy's standing there all pale with his fists clenched and a look on his face like I never saw. "They meant me. They says 'Jimmy' and then, 'Hi, dad.' "

I'm starting to feel sick myself. I kind of knew stuff was gonna happen. But, Jimmy was . . . I don't think Jimmy expected it, not so soon.

"Annie, how could anybody know? We ain't told no one yet."

Only Rainbow . . . and no way did R.B. say something. No way. So who?

We didn't even hear the car door slam. Jimmy's mom is standing there looking at me and then at Jimmy. And she's seeing the floor and the phone off the hook. Something about us, something about Jimmy's face stops her from letting him have it.

"Don't start, Mom." His voice is small and kinda tight. He's not yelling and he's not running out. He's just standing there looking like he's seen a ghost. His mom tosses him a sponge.

"Get that mess up before your father gets here."

I get a rag from under the sink. And me and Jimmy we're scrubbing away like it's gonna save us from something. His mom gives me a pat on the head. Nobody's saying nothing. Whoever was on the phone found out about it pretty quick.

Jimmy's mom is looking at the phone off the hook. She sticks leftover coffee in the microwave and zaps it. "Sit down, you two." She's looking at both of us.

"So who was that?"

Jimmy's always ragging on his mom, how she yells a lot, gives him crap and stuff about his room and the guys he runs with. I know she does it, but she's not doing it now. It's like we're grown-up or something. Frankie talked to her so I know she knows. I'm getting a little nervous. She really wants to talk.

"It's nothing, Mom!" Jimmy goes, real low, cool. I'm looking at him hard, but he's looking at the floor. His shoulders are getting tight.

"Jimmy!" His mom grabs his arm and pushes him back down. She's stronger than she looks.

"Jimmy, listen. This isn't easy. I know." She's looking at me like she really does know and I'm beginning to relax a little.

"People are gonna . . . people'll talk, wanna know what's up. We're all going to get the same. We gotta deal with it together."

Jimmy's not having any. He slams the door and starts running. In his workboots. He hasn't even got sneakers.

I know just what he's thinking. We been through

it so many times, how there's no way. Nothing to do.
How he's got a dumb job, no high school, no money,
how maybe his mom can take the baby, or one of
her sisters, or even Frankie. But then what happens
if we want the kid back? And the kid'll have parents,
I mean the guys who brought him up and stuff.
He might say, where you been, Dad? Why'd you
dump me?

So we give it away—our kid? Jimmy really swal-
lows hard when he talks about this part. That the kid
won't ever know we're the parents, that he was the
dad and that we really dug each other.

He told me he went home after. His feet just went
home like he wasn't thinking about it. He's dripping
sweat and his mom doesn't yell for once and his sister
ain't going like, "Ooh, ooh, that's disgusting." His
mom's just looking at him and he's going, "Yeah,
okay, Mom, you're uh . . . we'll talk. Later."

I'm cooking spaghetti, Frankie's coming, when the
doorbell rings. I really don't need anyone now. But
maybe it's Jimmy or my aunt. But they got keys, so
who?

Out the side window I see two brown heads, a
ponytail. Oh, mother of god, Bonnie and Nancy. Why
now? Oh, god, why now? I ain't together yet,
I . . . Another ring on the bell.

"I'm coming, just a second, okay?" I'm tying my hair up in a ponytail and my shirt is kind of, well, a little short and don't quite reach over the top of my jeans. I'm opening the door and Bonnie and Nancy are staring right at it, right at my stomach. Or are they? God, do they know or what?

"So we was walking on the way from Ray's Pizza. So we wanted to, you know, we thought we'd say hello or something," Nancy's saying.

"Like yeah," Bonnie goes. They both giggle.

"So how's school?"

"Oh yeah, that." Bonnie and Nancy start to giggle again.

"Tell her, Nancy," Bonnie says. "Tell her about Joey."

"There's this guy. He's in my typing class. He's so cute. He's got these incredible muscles and stuff and he plays football. We just started to go out. But he can't play unless he passes all his classes so he don't hang out too much. He asked me to the prom next week."

"And oh, the food. It's real yuck," Bonnie goes. "Totally disgusting. Nobody eats there and at lunchtime the whole place stinks. Mary says she got food poisoning."

"And the worst. You won't believe this, but they got these guards. They're not even as old as us, some of them, and they're supposed to protect us if there's trouble. But they don't even care. If you wanna get out, they say go on, go, we won't tell. Nobody's coming."

I'm sort of half listening to Bonnie and Nancy. I'm going, yeah, sure, uh huh, but I ain't there. It's like they're from another world and I want them to go.

They're not asking one thing about me. How I am or nothing. They seem so . . . with the prom and the football team and the cafeteria food . . . sort of far away. Like, who gives a damn—it's really different from the stuff I'm dealing with.

We used to hang out and laugh all the time. I can't think about what.

And all the time in back of my head, I'm thinking, do they know? Is it like Jimmy's phone call—they just came to look at me so's they can run around the neighborhood and blab about it? And they never even asked how I'm feeling, not even a how are you.

I might have, I just might have said something about it, if they asked, but they never did.

I'm sitting in the big stuffed chair that was Pop's. They get up to go and I say, "Just let yourselves out. I got to go to the bathroom."

I'm being awful, but I can't help it. They make me so mad. The door closes, and then they're giggling and running down the street. I'm half wishing I could be with Bonnie and Nancy and half knowing it won't ever be like that for me again.

7 *Frankie's driving the old Ford pickup and looking*
straight ahead. I'm thinking, who needs this?
How's a bunch of girls gonna help me? I'm
just fine. I don't need nothing.

Frankie's lips are so tight it looks like he got none
and he's holding on to the wheel like it's gonna save
his life.

"We're just trying it," he goes.

All the time Pop was sick, Frankie watched out for
me. He didn't like it, though. I got in his way . . . with
girls and stuff. And now this.

Frankie and Pop. Frankie was the oldest. But Kenny got married young and moved out. Frankie was Pop's favorite. Everybody said it. It was always my Frankie this and my Frankie that. Almost like brothers.

Pop liked to hear what Frankie was doing and where he was going, like to drag races and bars and stuff. I mean, when Pop was sick, Frankie was the one he wanted. Frankie made him laugh.

We get there, a small wooden house next to a fire station. I really want to blow this off.

A lady lets us in and I don't see nobody else. No big stomachs or nothing. We go into a room with a big brown desk and there're all these little pictures of babies on the walls, like a hundred babies or something.

And the whole place sort of smells funny, like a school cafeteria. There's a picture of a lady on the desk right in front of where I'm sitting, and she's bending over and kissing the hand of a bald old guy in a white dress.

Frankie sees me looking at it. "It's the Pope," he says. Like I don't know that, like I think it's some kind of drag queen.

A lady comes in and Frankie stands and kind of pushes me up, too, like we're saluting the flag or something. This stuff makes me nervous. People looking at me and talking to me like I was something just because I'm having a kid.

It's the same lady in the picture. She's smiling and holding out her hand to me and saying, "My name's Lu." Frankie's whispering under his breath, I'm sure the lady can hear him, how I gotta shake her hand.

Maybe she wants me to kiss it. I think these crazy things when I'm in this type of, you know, this type of deal. If I can think of something funny, like to kiss it, then I can get through.

But, Lu's smiling at me and looking okay like she doesn't hear Frankie. She's telling me I'm the client. I'm the main one—not my brother or my family or the baby.

And she's not going to tell me what to do. I got to make my own mind up about the baby, like what to do with it. I'm pretty sure I'm gonna give it away. But she keeps talking about this stuff like I gotta think what's the best thing for me and the kid. I gotta make a plan in case I change my mind and decide to keep it. Fat chance.

It's like the principal's office or the guidance counselor or something. But she's a social worker—a counselor or something.

She's got nice hair, sorta blonde and short and she smiles a lot and she's kind of quiet but, I don't know, like happy.

She's telling me and Frankie about a social worker who's going to work with us and help us find a home for the baby. I hear "social worker" and start thinking about R.B., how he got lucky with the cops after the fight with Dog Face. All they did was they gave him a social worker. I'm not sure what a social worker really does. And they're making him wash trains and under bridges and stuff, like it's a clean-up program or something. R.B., all he thinks about is his next hit.

"... files of people who want to adopt kids." I kind of tuned out. Lu's still talking something about how me and Jimmy can decide who we like and maybe even meet the family.

We gotta see the social worker once a week. It's a lot of bull to go through just to give up a kid. And papers to fill out about our families, do we have any diseases and stuff. The lady, uh, the social worker, will help us.

After me and Frankie talk to Lu, I go into a room next to Lu's office. Frankie goes in another room with a parent's group, even though he's my brother.

My group is girls who are thinking about giving away, I mean placing, their kids. Lu says you ain't giving away the baby, you're placing it.

There's a couch and lamps and a rug and stuff and a bunch of girls, some with bigger stomachs than me. That's not hard because even though I'm in my seventh month, you can hardly tell. I don't look fat. I only gained ten pounds so far.

Lu is saying I'm the new girl. This part I don't like.

They're telling me their names. I'm praying she don't ask me to say them back to her. Then she's asking everybody how they feel.

A girl called Cara's going how she already gave her baby—I mean placed it—like a month ago. So I don't get how come she's still coming here? Anyway she's talking like it was tough to do. In the hospital, no way did she want to see the baby or even touch it. So she tells the nurse. And then, she's going, well, I think I'll just take a look at her or I'll wonder what the kid looked like for the rest of my life.

It doesn't really hit her, she says, the whole thing, until the baby is born.

Yesterday she visits a friend's baby and starts to cry all over again. She's thinking how she can't go visit a baby without thinking about hers.

Cara can't keep the tears back. They're just coming. And Lu is saying it's okay. It's good to feel. Cara's trying to stop, but she just can't quit crying.

It's sort of awful and I begin to think I'm gonna start bawling myself. A couple of other girls are taking out Kleenex. It's like, like it would never end.

But, then, Cara's wiping her eyes and sitting very still. Nobody's saying anything, not Lu, not anybody. It's real quiet.

Cara goes, "I mean, I know this is for forever. But, I gotta keep thinking it's the best thing. I couldn't give that kid a life, not now and maybe not for a long time and then it would be too late. I gotta keep thinking that. Then I'm okay."

There's a feeling in the room after Cara spoke. I'm not sure what. Something happened, maybe just relief that she quit all that crying and stuff.

A girl called Inga is sitting on this brown folding chair. Her hair's so blonde it's almost white. She keeps running her fingers through it like she's combing it back, only it don't stay. She's eight months already and she's real big. Oh god, I hope I'm not gonna look like that, it's like she swallowed a bowling ball. Inga comes all the way from across some ocean from some place like Poland or China. She speaks funny, you can hardly understand her.

At first, she says, she loved the kid's father. He was her first boyfriend. Inga takes a piece of hair and twirls it around her finger like one of Kenny's kids with that dumb blanket he's always got—only Inga's fourteen. She sort of stops talking like she's looking into space and then she goes, "He swore he couldn't get me pregnant."

It's six months already, just like me, and she don't know anything. She begins to think something's wrong, missing periods and stuff. But she's never been regular. Her breasts are getting huge and hurting like mad. But even that . . .

One of the other girls goes, "Yeah, how do I know

something's whack just cause I'm getting these"—
she's waving her hands around in front of her chest—
"these bosoms. I never had a lot. . . . You know, no
tits. I thought, well, it's happening . . ." We're all kind
of laughing, even though it's not really funny or anything—it's just that we get what she's saying.

So Inga's going how she goes to check. They say,
Miss, you're pregnant. And she just can't believe it.
The guy lied to her. She didn't know and then it's
too late to do anything. She hates this guy. She ain't
had it yet, but she's saying no way she's gonna keep
this baby.

I'm thinking that me and Jimmy, we really like
each other. Jimmy's not just the father. Jimmy's my
friend.

Some of the girls got real mad when Lu called the
fathers the boyfriends. It was the only time she kind
of blew it. "Not the boyfriends," Cara says, "the fathers, birth fathers."

"Yeah," Inga says, "not boyfriends, no way."

So I'm not sure if it's harder when you love the
guy or hate him. I'm getting . . . I don't know, all this
stuff.

Someone else is talking—a sort of whisper from a
big armchair in the corner. I didn't hardly notice her.
Robin looks real young, like twelve or something,
except she's got on a ton of lipstick and she's got

these long red nails and her teeth—little white teeth—maybe all that lipstick makes her teeth look like that. She only had her kid last week.

So she comes home after the baby and her sisters look at the pictures she took in the hospital and say that's nice. But they don't get it. They want her to fool around and laugh and stuff the way she used to.

Robin's going how she was fine when she came home from the hospital until her oldest sister calls her a little girl—sort of like Frankie calling me Princess. She went nuts.

"They just don't get it." Robin's really mad, but she's crying.

And Lu's going how Robin had a kid, but nothing happened to her sisters. They're like they were before, so how're they gonna get it?

Frankly, I don't get a lot of the stuff Lu says, but there's something about the way she talks, like she knows she's right. She gets you thinking she is, too. She can tell how it's going to be, like she's a magician or something. And she says she's never even had a kid. I guess she's seen enough that has.

Everyone's quiet and Robin's looking at me and saying, "Annie, what about you? What's it like for you?"

I'm feeling a little, you know, kind of shy. But, then I'm saying, "It was after Pop died. I was sick a lot. I took Pop's death hard. I knew something was crazy right around, well, maybe March. It didn't even occur to me at first. I wasn't feeling so good, but I didn't do nothing.

"I'm thinking if I don't look at it and I think I'm not and dream I'm not, maybe I'm not. So I'm not doing nothing for six months. It's just like Inga. And now it's too late to get rid of it."

"So what're you gonna do?" Robin says.

"I'm not gonna keep it, that's for sure. That's all I know."

Cara says, "Is the father your boyfriend?"

"Yeah. He's my best friend."

"So?" goes Cara. "You and the boyfriend . . ."

"Jimmy," I say. "His name is Jimmy."

"So you and Jimmy are together. He's a good guy. Maybe you keep it."

"No way," I go. "We're too young. Jimmy's sixteen and I'm . . . I'm not even in school. I dropped out when Pop was sick. I took care of him."

"Do you think," Cara says, "if your dad was alive, what would he . . . what would he have—uh." Cara's looking at me. All the girls are really looking at me.

I never said this out loud before, not even to Frankie. "You know what Pop would've said? He'd want me to keep it.

"He'd never let me . . . he never . . . oh, god . . . If Pop was here, this whole thing, this whole thing—"

I'm losing it. I can feel myself going, but, it's too late—the tears are for Pop that I never cried, that I couldn't cry because I had to hold up, be grown-up. I'm crying for Pop. For the kid in my belly that I can't keep. After a while I feel arms around me and voices. Someone's patting me and there's a cup of tea in my hands. And I know I've been at it a long time.

Lu says if you don't let yourself feel, you know, sad and stuff, then the sadness don't go away. And you stay sad forever. It's really weird the way she says you gotta let yourself feel it, but then you gotta say *stop*. Like Robin says, she was crying and stuff and then she looked at her watch and timed herself. It's like . . . you gotta be two people. So she stopped crying and polished her nails.

8 *Lu asks me to come to the center for the thing they do with dolls. And I'm living here for a week* because Frankie says he can't drive me back and forth every day when he's on the road. And he don't want me on the bike with R.B.

So I'm in a room with some girls who've been here for two months already. I ain't used to hanging out with girls, but they're okay. They tell me they're keepin' their babies. One of them, Marie, is really big. She looks like she's gonna pop any minute, but

Doreen is small in front like me, even though she's due real soon.

This afternoon a social worker gave each of us a big doll and tells us how we gotta pretend it's a real baby. We can't go anywhere without it for a whole week. If we go out, we take it or else we gotta make arrangements like get a babysitter or something.

And we have to give the doll a name, like it's our kid. I decide to call mine Joey. Marie is calling hers Sam, even though it's a girl doll, and Doreen's is going to be Dorothy.

"Marie, your brother's here!" someone yells from downstairs.

About five minutes later, Marie comes running up and says, he's gonna take us to the lake, there's a fair up there. The bumper cars and merry-go-round are inside, so they go all winter. What do we think? Doreen and I look at each other. I guess we're both thinking about what to do with these crazy dolls. Doreen picks up Dorothy and puts her into her backpack with her head sticking out and I'm thinking yeah, I'll just wrap Joey in this scarf and tie it around my waist. Marie grabs Sam and we go downstairs giggling.

"Hey, Annie, this is my brother, Nick." Him and Doreen already met. Nick and I look at each other. "And, oh yeah, I'm forgetting—some guys you ain't met yet. Dorothy." She points to the yellow-haired doll in Doreen's pack. "And this is, um, oh, this is Joey. And this, tra-la, is your niece, Sam."

Nick is looking at us with this expression on his face, like he's thinking, I don't mind taking my sister and some friends to the fair, but these weirdo dolls are a little much. What if I meet some of the guys from work or something? I can't blame him. I feel pretty spaced myself.

Somehow we get piled into Nick's beat-up Ford and he's driving on the highway looking back every five minutes asking if we're all comfy with the "babies" and all. Now he's acting like it's a big joke. Sort of like we're all a big joke. The radio's blasting.

We go on the merry-go-round and the bumper cars. The bumpers are my favorite. Doreen's afraid, so I get in with her and I drive. We go faster and faster. I love to bump into people, to smash right into them. It's the greatest, because no matter how fast you go or where you hit the other guy, you know nothing bad's really gonna happen.

All of a sudden I hear someone yelling, "Stop, you gotta stop! I lost my kid, my kid fell out."

And I'm thinking, I have one awful moment where I'm thinking, god, what now? I turn around and there's Marie and she's out of her car and all the other cars are still racing around. Somehow the man don't hear her. And she's running to pick up her doll. And I'm thinking how Marie's gonna get hit. She's about to have a baby and she's gonna get hit. I drive to where she's bending down to sorta protect her from the other cars that are zooming all around and suddenly the power goes dead and everything's still.

The man who runs the place is running over to Marie and he's so mad.

"You dumb, stupid kids! You ain't gonna live too long if you do stupid stuff like that. All of you, outta here, outta here before I call the cops!"

He stands there looking really mean while Marie picks up her doll. Doreen and I try to keep our dolls out of sight as best we can while we walk across the floor with everybody watching. It feels like miles to the exit. People are beginning to snicker with our dolls and our stomachs and all.

Nick puts his arm around Marie and we go over to a hot dog stand. Marie and Doreen drink coke. I take chocolate milk and Nick has a beer.

"Hey, uh, Annie," he goes, "thanks. If you hadn't raced over and stopped in front of Marie she might've been, you know, she might've been . . ."

"It's okay," I go.

We're all walking along now, no one's saying much, but we feel like we've been through something, all of us. And somehow Nick's really part of it.

"Hey, let me hold a kid. How about it, Marie, can

I practice holding my niece?'' He grabs Sam and begins to run with her on his shoulders.

We all begin to run after him and Marie's yelling, ''Hey, she's too young, bring her back here this minute, Nicholas, or I'm gonna, I'm gonna . . .'' Nick is turning with the doll and tosses it back to Marie. She catches it by the leg. ''Whoops, sorry, honey,'' she goes to Sam.

Doreen tosses her doll to Nick. ''Take Dorothy for a ride, she's tough.'' Nick puts Dorothy under his arm like she's a football. I put Joey on my shoulders and begin to run after Nick. Down the path to the lake. Away from the fair. We're all running behind Nick waving these stuffed pieces of cloth.

The Dorothy doll is losing her stuffing and her leg is sticking out at a strange angle. But Nick doesn't notice. He keeps running. We all keep running and laughing and bumping into each other and dropping the stupid dolls and tossing them to each other right up to the edge of the water. We're sitting in a heap on the ground with our bottoms wet, but it don't matter. For the first time in a long time, it seems like everything's okay. I can breathe again. I feel real.

''Hey, guys, look at Dorothy,'' Doreen goes.

Nick takes a look at the leg. ''Looks like a major break. Gotta go to the hospital.''

But Doreen is really upset about what to tell the

social worker and Lu. All the dolls are pretty wet and Dorothy is a mess.

"Hey, guys, I got it." Marie is standing on a rock. We're all lying flat on the sand and Marie's belly sticks out so far we can hardly see her head.

At exactly that second, when we're all staring at Marie and waiting to hear how she's gonna get us out of this, I feel an awful twinge. Like I'm having a bad period or something and then something warm and gushy goes down my leg. I bend my knees and put my hands over my stomach. Oh, god, I think I'm having it! I'm having it!

Doreen and Nick lift me up and are half dragging me and half carrying me along the beach back to the car. About every five minutes, I'm getting this intense pain in my stomach and I just have to stop walking, but then it stops and I can move again.

I'm back in the car. Someone has thrown an old blanket over me. I can see the dolls out of the corner of my eye in a heap. Marie remembered. Nick is driving fast and I hear him muttering under his breath. "Come on, car. Come on, God. If You get me through this, I promise I'll be the best kid on the block. I'll do anything You say. Just let me get her there on time. Just this once, God, give me a break."

Nick screeches to a stop at a red light. Flashing lights pull up behind him. A car door slams.

"Let's see that license, boy." A cop pokes his head

in the window and takes one look at me and the next thing I know we're whizzing through traffic.

I hear a siren blowing and the red flashing light's in front of us now and we're going so fast that if I wasn't feeling this bad, I'd be scared to death. But I'm scared to death anyway. I thought I'd have more time. I thought I'd see Jimmy and we'd go to the hospital together and now all this is happening and there's no more time.

9 *The nurse is standing over me. I guess she don't* know she's supposed to ask me. To ask whether I want to see my baby and hold it. They're supposed to do that when the baby's up for adoption. And here she is with the baby in her arms.

"Here's your girl, Mrs. Easter." She's pushing the blanket in front of my nose. I can't not take it. Oh, god.

The next day, they must have heard about me because they aren't bringing the baby out at feeding time. But when I walk down to the end of the hall and see only one baby in the nursery all alone, I run to the nurses' station and say, "Get her out, get her out right now."

Jimmy arrives with Frankie and Kenny and my aunt and we're all looking at the baby and for a little while, I pretend—not pretend, really, but just forget about stuff and act like the baby's going to be ours. And that we can keep her forever.

Frankie and everybody go out to talk to the nurses or have a cigarette or something and Jimmy and me hold the kid. The family for the adoption, we almost couldn't decide, but two sounded cool. They both wanted a kid real bad. We really cared about that part—that they would really love her. And we wanted lots of pets—dogs and cats and stuff and her own room.

But one family wrote how the mom teaches art and says how they're really into it, and music, too. We picked that one. Maybe the kid'll grow up to be kind of like Rainbow and do comics or make pictures or something. The family wanted to meet us, but Jimmy didn't want to. He said no. Someday maybe we can tell her how we felt if she don't hate us for giving her—for placing her.

The social worker says it's a good idea to name the baby, so that when we think about her we can call her something instead of just "it" or "her."

When Frankie and Kenny come back, Frankie says

if we gotta name the baby, let's name it after Mom. Jimmy and me look at each other. Jimmy sorta touches my arm and looks at the kid, "Yeah, sounds right."

So Frankie says, "She's Emily. Little Emily." He picks up her hand and kisses it. Kenny squeezes Emily's foot. Everyone's sort of, well, we're looking at each other, like, I don't know, like . . . it feels kinda strange and sad, like what're we doing this for?

Frankie goes, "I need a cigarette. The truck, it's, uh, it's . . . I'm gonna get towed. See you tomorrow, old buddy." Frankie kisses me on the top of my head.

Kenny pats my arm. And my aunt—like she got tears in her eyes or else her makeup is running—gives me a kiss. They split and me and Jimmy hold each other for a few minutes. He says I smell like Emily, sort of powdery and milky. I tell him he smells like a garage.

Then I'm looking at Jimmy, right in his face, in his eyes. "You think she'll have those? Those baby blues? My hair, your eyes—she'll be something!"

Jimmy is hugging me again very hard, harder than before. It's making my chest hurt. It's my milk. They gave me shots to get rid of it, but I still hurt.

"Oh, Annie!"

We got our arms around each other's shoulders and our foreheads pressed together. We're looking at each other, like our eyes are stuck. It's like we're seeing inside each other. It's like we're seeing . . . I'm not sure what we're seeing. It's so still I can hear the heartbeat of the fetal heart monitor connected to the girl in the room next to me. She hasn't had hers yet. They say she's late.

Me and Jimmy. We're . . . we ain't speaking. No words. If we speak, we might start bawling. Then I feel his body tense. I can tell he's gonna split, go running, find Rainbow and go bombing, I don't know what. But I know he just has to get out of here. I'd go too, if I could.

I'm lying in bed with my eyes closed, this is really heavy stuff, it makes me so tired. Voices in the hall. For a second I think I hear Rainbow, but I know it ain't. He already told me he hates hospitals.

I open my eyes and see Doreen and Marie and Nick standing around my bed looking so serious.

"About those dolls," I go. We look at each other and begin laughing.

Nick hands me a bunch of daisies. "From all of us, for you and the kid."

"For me and Emily."

"For you and Emily," they say after me.

It's really good to see them. It's like we've always known each other, even though all we did was ride bumper cars and stuff. I guess it was sort of a big deal getting to the hospital and all. Marie says that the doctors are thinking about inducing labor because she's overdue.

"Nick, can you imagine if we'd all started to have our babies the other day?" I go. Nick makes like he's gonna faint.

"That cop, man, was he scared. Just a rookie. Said he's never done a delivery before and he was praying harder than me that we'd make it to the hospital on time."

Was that only the other day? God, it seems like years ago. And Nick and Marie and Doreen. It's as if we've known each other forever. Like they're my good friends. Maybe forever don't have to take a long time.

The nurse comes in and says that visiting hours are over. Time to go. She's leaving and then she's turning around and saying how she forgot to give me something, a roll of paper or something. She don't know what.

It's like a brown bag from the supermarket, only it's a piece of paper, the longest piece of paper I ever saw, longer than my bed. They're unrolling this thing, Doreen and Nick. It says JIMMY, ANNIE, EMILY, in pink spray paint. With a big heart around it. We're looking at this thing and I'm thinking, Rainbow.

Tomorrow the social worker comes to take Emily away. I don't want tomorrow to ever get here. I hate the social worker. When everyone is out the door, I start to cry. I've never felt so alone in my life. Not ever.

10 *GET READY! GET SET! GO! in big red letters.* The instructions freak me out—I got the clock set and I'm in GO. I'm gonna be a redhead, like they say Ma was—maybe Emily's gonna be, too. When I . . . if I ever see her, I'll have to tell her mine ain't real. God, I need more towels. I'm gooping this mess that looks like red shaving cream all over my head. If it's so nothing, how come I gotta wear these crazy gloves that fit me about as good as Frankie's socks.

Jimmy must've come home with Frankie cause

they're both standing at the bathroom door looking at me in my old T-shirt and cut-off jeans. I can't tell if Frankie's pissed or if they just think I look funny with this red fingerpaint stuff all over my head. I'm going, "I'm in GO." They don't get it—that I'm in the middle of timing this stupid thing, and I can't stop now or I'll get messed up, too red or something.

They're still standing there like they don't know what's happening so I'm squeezing out more goop and making like if they don't get out, I'm gonna goop them next. Jimmy makes a grab for Frankie's shaving cream—like we're gonna have a foam fight.

Frankie's got this face on and he's shaking his head like he don't get girls or like he thinks I lost it, but I can tell he's glad to see us kidding around. He closes the door and I hear the frig opening and the TV on.

Jimmy's behind me and got his arms around my waist. We gotta write to the kid—what Lu was talking about for when she grows up—so she'll know about me and Jimmy, but I ain't saying nothing. Jimmy's rubbing my back and sticking his nose into my neck. And I'm going, "Just let me finish this mess." I stick my head under the faucet and all the red stuff is running into the sink. I got the washcloth over my eyes and feel a little like I'm drowning.

What if the parents don't tell the kid, and never give her our letter and the locket we're gonna buy. If they're like me, if I'm scared or something, I ain't always honest. Oh god, like right this minute, our kid is in a house someplace and they're giving her a bath . . . hugging her, loving her. I can't think about it. I just can't. The water's running clear. What do I do now? Oh yeah, the conditioner. It's like what Cara says, she couldn't give the kid a life—me and Jimmy neither, not for a long time and then it'd be too late.

I miss those nights with Lu when she'd say stuff like you gotta feel. You gotta let yourself feel the pain, that's what she'd say. That part's easy. But how do you make it quit?

Oh my god, it's really red. I look like what's her name—that actress Pop always talked about, Rita somebody with the red hair.

Frankie's going, "Annie, what's up? The spaghetti's hot."

And I'm—I can't. I don't know if I can go out there. I look so not me—like I don't know who. I open the door.

At our house, we always just take from the pot and go sit anywhere—like in front of the TV or in our room, but tonight they got the table set and flowers.

Jimmy's looking at me. Frankie's looking, too. Then Frankie gets up and comes over to where I'm standing. For a second, I'm scared he's gonna hit me. But he takes my arm like I'm Sunny or a grown-up or something and he's kinda hugging my shoulder and pulling out the chair for me to sit.

And Jimmy's going, "Yeah . . . it's okay. It's cool."

Frankie's passing the plates loaded with spaghetti and tomato sauce that looks like—well, it's red, like my hair.

Jimmy's trying to eat slow. He usually eats fast. He's cutting the meatballs in little pieces. I'm seeing myself in this mirror behind Jimmy—like who is that?—I still ain't sure, but I think I dig it. Frankie's drinking his beer and slurping up his spaghetti like always and I'm going, we gotta write that letter to Emily . . . for when she grows up.

Second Thoughts

Chapter 10 Revisited

"Are you okay, Hon?" The nurse is talking to me in that phony happy voice they all got. Like this is the greatest thing in the world or something. She's sticking the tray with the pills under my nose—pink pills for sleeping and little green pills to keep me relaxed. I slide them to the side of my mouth and concentrate on not swallowing. I'm trying to look like I'm "okay, Hon."

The nurse is fixing my pillows and lowering the bed and making dumb conversation. All I can think is if she don't get out of here soon I'm going to gag with these pills stuffed into my cheek. She walks just before I explode and spit the whole gray mess into a glass. My mouth burns, but I don't care. I only care about getting Emily and getting out of here.

I been planning it—since after I had Emily. I don't give a damn about the social worker. I feel a little bad about Lu, the time we spent talking, that conversation the time she tells me how I gotta see two sides, how I gotta play it both ways in my head and think what it would be like to keep the kid. I ducked that one. I thought, it's impossible. No way I keep the kid.

I keep hearing Cara saying how she can't even visit a friend's baby without crying, thinking of the kid she gave up. ''Gave up!'' Not all that ''place the baby'' bull that the social worker was always laying on us. No one oughtta ache that much. Not Cara, not me and Jimmy, nobody. And it don't matter whether you love the guy or hate him. The kid is something else. The kid's a whole new life.

God, when they handed Emily to me, I never felt like that, ever. My own kid—from my body—part of Mom and Pop and Jimmy and me. I just ain't doing it. No way am I gonna do it.

Even if Jimmy hates me, or wants to kick me off, I'll explain it. I'll make a plan, get a job, I don't know, something. There's gotta be a way. I could work at

Rosie's. Or maybe Frankie knows someone. Pop would've understood. I know he would've.

No one's on duty, just one nurse. And it's pretty dark. This dump has no money so they turn off most of the lights at night. I wait for someone to push a call button. It feels like hours and then I see a winking red dot down the hall in the opposite direction from the baby station. It's perfect. I got on my old raincoat. The black skirt I came in with is all crumpled up in my shoulder bag. And Rainbow's paper roll. I gotta have that.

I tip-toe down the hall to the nursery—all these babies in little white cribs. Emily's sleeping real good. I pick her up and check her wristband to make sure it's my kid. I wrap her in the skirt. Her mouth and nose stick out good so she can breathe. I put her into my bag and sneak down the stairs to the side door. This place isn't run too hot. I'm saying a prayer for both of us.

The street's dark and no one's around. I'm walking, running, falling over my sneakers a little, even though I know the way. It helps to live in a place a long time. The street's all empty. I smell beer and coffee before I see the sign: BEN'S BAR.

I'm thinking, Rosie's. Yeah, that great coffee smell real early and everybody saying good morning. I'll bring Emily in one of them backpacks. Some creeps in front of Ben's begin talking to me. Then they see

I'm carrying a kid and start to say rude things. I just hold Emily tighter and keep going.

I'm okay for the first time in ages. It's like when you're a kid, the way your breath gets knocked out of you when you fall down hard, the way you can't breathe. You're gasping for air. You think you're dying for sure. And, then suddenly it's okay. Your chest begins to move and you can breathe again. That's how I feel right this minute. That's the way it is for me right now. I can breathe again.

I'm walking along listening to my footsteps in the dark, thinking about me and Emily—whether her hair's gonna be red like Mom's and curly like mine, whether her eyes are gonna stay blue. I hear a humming sound, a motorcycle, getting louder. I hold Emily close to me and walk faster. I ain't scared, not really.

The bike's still coming. It takes a minute before I recognize that little click in the engine. I know that bike. Rainbow says every bike has its own hum. I turn around fast, but it's just a guy on a Harley. He doesn't pass me, he turns before he reaches where I am. I'm sort of scared, but more relieved than scared—just to be out of the hospital with Emily. I don't hurt at all. I could go forever. I'm just a little sticky between my legs.

The bike's next to me, roaring in my ears. It's dark, and I can't see the driver with his helmet and stuff.

The visor's covering his face. I look over at the bike. I'm not seeing anyone I know. And then I hear Rainbow laughing.

"I came back on a hunch, Annie, I know you pretty good. But I didn't see nobody. I almost kept going. Something made me come back again."

Rainbow's Mom is touching Emily the way she touched my face the first time we met. She's holding her so gentle and cooing at her. Rainbow has us laughing how the guys at the 7-Eleven asked him if he had a kid or something when he went in to buy diapers. Tomorrow we'll call Frankie and Jimmy and deal with the hospital. But, tonight, it's me and Emily and nobody knows where I am.

THINK ABOUT IT

A few generations ago we all experimented with sex, but nobody talked about it. If asked, you'd swear you'd never even kissed a boy, never mind going to bed with him. It was a different time. If you did it, you didn't tell.

Today, times have changed, but the question remains: If you get pregnant, what do you do?

Although *Baby Blues* is a novel, it's about real people faced with tough choices. In Chapter Five, Annie knows she has a problem and asks Beanie to help her find Frankie. Frankie listens to Annie and then calls her "a great big stupid jerk." He's angry not because she's pregnant but because she didn't trust him enough to tell him right away. That's what really hurts him, that she didn't think she could talk to him. Annie's lucky because Frankie is there for her.

In "Second Thoughts" Annie discovers how hard it is to see yourself in a situation before you get there. Even after Frankie's help, and talks with Lu, and the stuff with the dolls, in "Second Thoughts," Annie is unprepared for the depth of her feelings about Emily. It takes her completely by surprise.

Girls most successful in dealing with an unexpected pregnancy are those who prepare by carefully considering all possibilities. So, if you had a friend like Annie, the best thing would be to encourage her to talk about it with someone who would understand, someone trustworthy—a close friend, the parent of a friend, or if possible, her own parents. Even if it's hard. For some kids, it's easier to talk to someone they don't know, people who are trained to help, like a counselor, therapist, or minister.

Whatever the decision, it has to come from thinking about all sides of the situation. Nobody can or should decide for somebody else. It's your friend's life, her body, and it will be her kid. No matter what happens, she is the one who will have to live with the decision.

ABOUT THIS BOOK

They wanted a baby and couldn't have one of their own. So they went to a place where there were babies that needed parents. They walked through rooms with many cribs with babies in them. One baby, me, grabbed my daddy's hand and wouldn't let go. He and my mom thought I was the cutest, cuddliest thing they ever saw. They loved me right away. They decided that I was the baby they would take home to be their very own child.

This is the story I was told one afternoon just before my fifth birthday. The shades of my room were pulled and I was sitting on my mom's lap. In those days most five-year-olds had no clue where babies came from. I thought it might be the stork. But after my mom spoke, I knew that no matter how other kids got the moms and dads they had, the way I got mine was somehow different. I wasn't like other kids. The worst part was that my mom was scared when she was telling me this story. I realize now that it was because she was afraid I wouldn't love her anymore or that I might be angry at her. I remember asking if she was okay and hugging her.

After that, except for my best friend in kindergarten, I never mentioned the story about the way my family found me to another living person. When I was a teenager, the social worker and people from the adoption agency told my parents to talk to me about the adoption again. They said this was important for my development.

My parents left newspaper articles in my room about children who had been adopted, but they never talked about it directly. It was still a difficult subject for them and I knew it. When I found these articles, I behaved very strangely. Part of me really wanted to talk about it and another part of me would get furious. I would yell at my parents and say things like, "Why are you leaving this stupid, boring stuff around? I don't give a damn about this!" Of course this wasn't the whole truth. But nobody seemed to understand that another side of me would do almost anything to talk about it. The adoption agency told my parents that if it didn't seem to make any difference to me, to forget it.

For a long, long time I stopped asking questions altogether. When I finally grew up and became wiser, I realized that it was all right to question where I had come from. I discovered that my parents didn't mind, they welcomed it. They told me everything they remembered about the facts of the adoption, but they didn't know who my biological parents were or how I could find them.

At that time all adoption records in New York State were sealed. Information is more easily available now, but the laws are different from state to state.

Ten years ago, after a long search, I found my biological family: my father and a full brother who looks exactly like me—only he has a moustache. My biological mother had died many years before.

This story about Annie and Jimmy comes from thinking a lot about what it must have been like for my biological mom and dad—how they must have felt giving up a child.

H. H .W.

WHERE TO FIND INFORMATION

The Resource Guide on the next pages offers pregnant teens ideas about where to turn to for information, advice, and support. You might also try looking in the Yellow Pages of your local telephone directory, under Social and Human Services. Key words to look for are: Abortion Alternatives, Abortion Counseling, Services for Single Parents, Unmarried Parents, Teen Parents, Sex Information and Educational Counseling, Teen Mothers, Teen Fathers, or Women's Health Services.

Hospitals have teen and community outreach programs, as do many religious organizations. Many organizations are helpful once they understand the situation. If they can't help, they often recommend groups that can.

Keep trying. Don't be discouraged if the first phone call doesn't produce the needed information.

In New York City, the YWCA has a program for teen parents, birth fathers, and birth mothers which provides day-care, preparation for the GED (a high school equivalency diploma), classes in parenting, job training, and support groups. There is a waiting list. When I asked the teen mothers there how they learned about the program, they said it was mostly through word-of-mouth, networking. Other ways mentioned were school counselors, shelters, and friends who had been there. One woman said that she worked across the street and had seen young people coming in with babies.

If adoption is a possibility, there are adoption networks, birth-parent suppport groups, national and international registries for adoptions, newspaper listings, and listings on the computer Internet.

A mother of two recently adopted children told me that a qualified agency will help birth mothers consider all alternatives, not only adoption, so that she will be confident with her decision. But while you make your decision it is important to realize that adoption agencies are not neutral. They are looking for healthy babies for adoptive parents.

Most agencies are available to answer phone calls at all times of the day and night. The law provides a waiting period before an adoption becomes final, in case the birth mother changes her mind as Annie does in "Second Thoughts."

RESOURCE GUIDE

It may be helpful to review this guide and/or contact any agency or service in the company of a trusted friend.

RECOMMENDED BOOKS

Krementz, Jill. *How It Feels To Be Adopted.* New York: Knopf, 1982.

Lifton, Betty Jean. *Twice Born.* New York: Penguin Books, 1977.

———. *Tell Me a Real Adoption Story.* New York: Knopf, 1994.

Rappaport, Bruce. *The Open Adoption Book: A Guide to Adoption Without Tears.* New York: Macmillan, 1992.

Services for Young Fathers: A New York State Directory, 1995–1996. New York: YWCA, 1995.

Solinger, Rickie. *Wake Up Little Susie: Single Pregnancy and Race Before* **Roe v. Wade.** New York: Routeledge, 1992.

Strauss, Jean. *Birthright: A Guide to Search and Reunion for Adoptees, Birthparents and Adoptive Parents.* New York: Penguin, 1994.

PERIODICALS

AdoptNet Magazine
P.O. Box 50514
Palo Alto, CA 94303-0514

Birthparents Newsletter
3424 Blue Rock
Cincinnati, OH 45239

USA Today: In this nationally distributed newspaper adoption listings can be found in the Life section under "Marketplace Today." A typical ad might say:
   "We will provide a wonderful home and bright future. Expenses paid."
Included are the full names of the family and an 800 phone number. Here, as elsewhere, it's important to check the credentials of the agency or the lawyers that you are dealing with by contacting either the American Academy of Adoption Lawyers or the National Adoption Information Clearinghouse (listed below).

AGENCIES, SUPPORT GROUPS, REFERRALS, REGISTRIES

The Adoption Center. See National Federation for Open Adoption: The Adoption Center.

Adoption Services Associates
8703 Wurzbach Road
San Antonio, TX 78240
Tel: (210) 699-6094 or
       (800) 648-1807

American Academy of Adoption Lawyers
P.O. Box 33053
Washington, DC 20033-0053
Tel: (803) 723-1688
This organization will provide a national directory
of member attorneys. It is suggested that adoptive
and biological parents have separate attorneys so
that each will have their own interests fully repre-
sented.

Adoptees' Liberation Movement Association
(ALMA)
P.O. Box 727
Radio City Station
New York, NY 10101
Tel: (212) 581-1568
An organization in New York City with branches in
other cities across the country. ALMA helps adopted
people eighteen years old and over learn how to
search for their biological families. ALMA also works
with biological parents. The organization maintains
a national registry of adoptive and biological families.
If both parties are registered, families are able to find
each other immediately.

Catholic Human Services (formerly Community,
Family and Children Services)
1000 Hastings Street
Traverse City, MI 49686
Tel: (616) 947-8110

*Concerned United Birthparents National Head-
quarters*
2000 Walker Street
Des Moines, IA 50317
Tel: (800) 822-2777

Council for Equal Rights in Adoption
401 E. 74th Street
New York, NY 10021
Tel: (212) 988-0110
This referral source and educational organization
represents 337 adoption agencies worldwide. It offers
mental health facilities, counseling, and support
groups for people involved in adoption.

Independent Adoption Center. *See* National Feder-
ation for Open Adoption: The Adoption Center.

International Soundex Reunion Registry (ISRR)
P.O. Box 2312
Carson City, NV 89702
Tel: (702) 882-7755
A free information registry for those who are search-
ing for next of kin. Send self-addressed stamped
envelope.

Internet Resources
If you have access to computer Internet, you can use
WorldWide Web. Start with a Web browser. Look
for key words as you would in the Yellow Pages of
your telephone directory. From key words like *pregnant, adopt, abortion, discuss, health, teenager, women*,
look for connections to other resources.

Louise Wise Adoption Agency
12 East 94th Street
New York, NY 10128
Tel: (212) 876-7143
An adoption agency that offers services, including a
recently developed Teen Father Program, for children
and parents.

National Adoption Center Hot Line
Tel: (800) TO ADOPT (862-3678)

National Adoption Information Clearinghouse
5640 Nicholson Lane, Suite 300
Rockville, MD 20852
This service is very informative and helpful. If you
leave a message, your call will be returned. Information is offered on support groups, computer networks, and general adoption procedures, such as
how to request a home study of a prospective adoptive family from the Department of Public Welfare.

National Council for Adoption
1930 17th Street NW
Washington, DC 20009
Tel: (202) 328-8072
    (800) 333-NCFA (6232)
A national organization that helps to set guidelines
and policy on adoption. They have lists of licensed
child placement member agencies in almost every
state. They handle international placement, and special needs children, and provide counseling and other
social services.

National Federation for Open Adoption: The Adop-
tion Center (formerly the Independent Adoption
Center
391 Taylor Boulevard, Suite 100
Pleasant Hill, CA 94523
Tel: (510) 827-2229 or
8616 La Tijera Boulevard, Suite 212
Los Angeles, CA 90045
Tel: (310) 215-3180 or
    500 E. Washington Street, Suite 200
Muncie, IN 47305
Tel: (800) 771-3721 or (800) 877-OPEN (6736)

Offices to open in July 1995 in Atlanta, Georgia.
This referral network promotes open adoption and
encourages an ongoing relationship between the
birth parents and the adoptive family. An adoption
education program counsels birth mothers at the organization's expense before the birth and for a year
or more after the birth, if necessary. This group can
put you in touch with birth parent support groups
nationwide.

Planned Parenthood of America, Federation of
For a clinic near you, call (800) 230-PLAN (7526).
Services vary according to geographic area, but all
offer confidential, non-judgmental advice about your
options.

Women's Health Line
Tel:(212) 230-1111
The phone is answered by a human being, not a
machine, who will tell you about programs and services offered in the area in which you live. They have
many programs for teenagers and offer information
on Medicaid, birth control, abortion, and parenting.

YWCA
610 Lexington Avenue
New York, NY 10022
Services for Young Families
Tel: (212) 735-9784
Young Fathers' Program
Tel: (212) 735-9773
Teen Programs for birth mothers and fathers offer
classes in parenting, job training, preparation for the

GED (high school equivalency diploma), day care, and support groups.

You can order a copy of *Services for Young Fathers: A New York State Directory, 1995–96* by writing to the YMCA or by phoning (212) 735-9737.

GLOSSARY

ADOPT   "To take by free choice into a close relationship previously not existing, especially by a formal legal act; specifically: to take voluntarily a child of other parents to be in the place of or as one's own child."*

CLOSED ADOPTION   A legal process of adoption in which records are sealed, birth certificates are altered and neither family knows who the other is.

OPEN ADOPTION   A legal process by which the biological parents decide with a social worker who the adoptive parents will be. Adoptive parents and biological parents meet: the adoptive parents may be present at the birth of the baby, and the biological parents may have visiting rights that are worked out and agreed upon in advance by both parties.

*From *Webster's Third New International Dictionary*.

PARTIALLY OPEN ADOPTION A legal process by which the biological parents select the family in which the baby is to be placed and send information to be given to the child when he/she is eighteen years old. Each family knows who the other one is.

Helen Keller was a famous author who could not see or hear.
Helen traveled all around the world.
She shared her stories about learning how to read, write, and speak.
She inspired and helped many people.

In 1937, Helen Keller sailed
on a ship from America to Japan.
It was her very first time
traveling to Asia.

A blind man named Takeo Iwahashi
(say: ta-KAY-o ee-wa-HA-shee)
had invited Helen to Japan.
Like Helen, he wanted to help
other people like him.
He printed many books in braille
(say: BRAYL) so that blind people
could read and learn.

The Japanese people loved listening to Helen's speeches. Helen spoke about peace, respect, and understanding other people's differences.

Helen also had a special request
while she was in Japan.
She wanted to meet
an Akita (say: ah-KEE-tuh) dog!

The Akita is a dog breed
from Japan.
Ever since she was a little girl,
Helen had loved dogs.
She had owned many dogs,
but she had never owned an Akita.

Helen had read about the true story
of the Akita named Hachikō
(say: ha-chi-KOH).
Every evening Hachikō met his
owner at the train station.
But one day Hachikō's owner
did not come home after work.

More trains came and left.
Hachikō waited and waited,
but his owner never appeared.

Helen was inspired by Hachikō
and his loyalty.
She wanted to meet an Akita dog.
She met a small puppy
that she nicknamed "Kami"
(say: KAH-mee).

The next day Hachikō went
to the station again.
He went the next day, and the next.
For more than nine years
Hachikō didn't give up looking
for the person he loved.

Kami licked Helen's cheek
and cuddled in her lap.
"May I keep him?"
Helen asked.
Kami's owner said yes!

Kami traveled with Helen
to his new home in New York.
He became the first Akita
to live in the United States.

But a few months later
Kami died from a virus
that affects some dogs.
Helen was very sad.

The Japanese people were also
sad to hear about Kami's death.
Kami had connected Helen to
Japan, but now he was gone.
The Japanese people had an idea.
They would send another dog
to Helen!

Kenzan-Go (say: ken-zahn-GO),
or "Go-Go,"
was Kami's brother.

Go-Go was bigger than Kami,
but he was just as friendly.
He would be the perfect fit
for Helen!

But there was a problem.
Trouble was brewing between
Japan and the United States.

Back in 1922 both countries had promised to stop building new battleships. They wanted to focus on peace, not war.

But as time went on,
Japan changed its mind.
It started building new battleships.

Americans were worried.
Japan's army and navy were growing.
The US president was not sure
if he could trust Japan.

Some people in Japan were scared
that Go-Go's trip would be unsafe.
No one knew what would happen
with all the trouble and distrust.

Go-Go was still ready
to meet Helen.
His ship left Japan
in the beginning of June 1939.

The journey was long and far. Go-Go's ship was surrounded by blue ocean and blue sky.

Finally the ship arrived in
New York.

Would Go-Go be allowed
off the ship?

"Welcome to America!"
the guard said.
And there was Helen Keller,
standing on the pier!

Go-Go ran to his new owner
and gave her a big doggy kiss.
Helen laughed.
They were so happy
to be with each other.

Helen was very grateful for the gift.
When Helen was with Go-Go,
she remembered all the kind people
she had met in Japan.

No matter what happened,
Helen would always think of
the Japanese people as her friends.
Go-Go lived a long and happy life
with Helen Keller.
Nothing could separate an
Akita and its owner.

· Facts About Akita Dogs ·

- Akitas are strong and powerful. They used to be popular hunting dogs!
- Akitas get their name from the Akita region in northern Japan.
- Akitas have webbed toes. This makes it easier for them to walk on snow.
- In Japan the Akita dog is considered a national treasure.
- Hachikō is still very famous today. Movies have been made and books have been written about his story. In Tokyo there is also a famous Hachikō statue at the Shibuya (say: shee-BU-ya) train station. The statue is a popular meeting spot.

· Facts About Helen Keller ·

- Helen Keller was born on June 27, 1880, and died on June 1, 1968.
- She became blind and deaf when she was nineteen months old.
- Helen was the first blind and deaf person to graduate from college.
- Helen traveled to Japan with her companion, Polly Thomson. One of the ways they communicated with each other was spelling words onto the other person's palm.
- Helen visited Japan again in 1948 and 1955.